D1006024

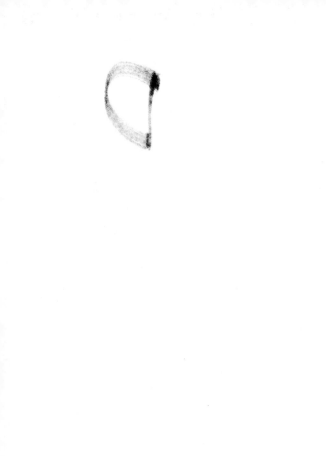

# The Lighthouse Mermaid

### Kathleen Karr

ILLUSTRATED BY KAREN LEE SCHMIDT

Hyperion Books for Children

NEW YORK

To Trish,
*For the sage advice—*
*and the mermaids!*
—K. K.

Text © 1998 by Kathleen Karr.
Illustrations © 1998 by Karen Lee Schmidt.

Printed in the United States of America.

First Edition

1 3 5 7 9 10 8 6 4 2

The artwork for this book is prepared using pencil.
The text for this book is set in 16-point Berkeley Book.

Library of Congress Cataloging-in-Publication Data

Karr, Kathleen.
The lighthouse mermaid / Kathleen Karr ; illustrated by Karen Lee Schmidt.
p.   cm.
Summary: Kate, who lives in a lighthouse and often dreams that she is a mermaid, has
a chance to rescue two real mermaids one stormy night.
ISBN 0-7868-2297-X (lib. bdg.) — ISBN 0-7868-1232-X (pbk.)
[1. Mermaids—Fiction.  2. Lighthouse—Fiction.]  I. Schmidt, Karen, ill.
II. Title.
PZ7.K149Li     1998
[Fic]—dc21
97-37367

# Contents

# CHAPTER ONE

# The Island

Last night I dreamed I was a mermaid.

It was a lovely dream. My world was all blue and green, my favorite colors. I swam between strands of seaweed. My hair flowed behind me. Long and thick it flowed, like honey. I turned my head and laughed. The laughter bubbles floated above my tail. It was the most wondrous tail, with scales that shone like silver and gold. I flipped it and rose to the surface. There was my island, waiting for me. It was all golden, too, shining brighter than the sun.

Then I woke up.

The golden sun had disappeared.

Three seconds later it returned. Once more it was gone. I sighed. It was only the beam from the light high above me. Between its regular flashes I knew it was still night. I crawled from my warm quilts and touched my nose to the cold window. How pretty the icy fairy patterns were. It was winter on my lighthouse island. But in my dreams it was always summer.

I shivered as the beam came again. Time to crawl back under my quilts. If I tried very hard, maybe the dream would return.

My eyes closed against the sudden darkness.

I was late to breakfast.

"Kate!" Mama turned from the big black stove. "You've been lying abed with your dreams again. And me left with all your chores!"

"I'm sorry, Mama. But it was such a perfect dream—"

Mama sniffed and hung on to her

stomach. She was very big with child. Again. "And how your imaginary sea creatures will be helping you in this cold world—"

I didn't answer. How could I tell her that mermaids were my only friends? How could I explain that sometimes I wished I *were* a mermaid? She wouldn't understand. Not Mama, with all her children to care for. Not Papa, either, always in the tower with his light. And surely not my four younger brothers and sisters. Weren't they part of what the mermaids helped me to escape from? I sat to table between two brothers and reached for my bowl. It was cornmeal mush. Again.

"Pass the molasses, Joel."

"Gone," he said.

"Gone? You've eaten it all?"

"Davey got the last drop!" He stuck out his tongue at my other brother.

"How could you, Davey!"

"Hush, Kate. And put that tongue where it belongs, Joel." Mama poured me some milk. "That's not all that's gone. Or almost gone. You know the lighthouse tender is overdue these three months." She tried not to look worried. "Be thankful we have the cow and hens." She watched me stuff down the mush. "And they're overdue for feeding."

"Why can't the boys do it sometime?"

Mama's voice was stern. "You are the biggest and oldest, Kate. You're nearly eleven. There's another nor'easter coming, too. It could sweep the boys clear into the sea."

I scowled. Mermaids didn't have to tend cows and hens. Mermaids didn't have useless little brothers. Or little sisters, either. I glanced at the twins in their crib by the stove. Patience was napping already. Prudence was trying to walk. She tumbled into her twin. A howl set up.

I went for my cloak and boots. At least it would be quiet in the shed.

\* \* \*

It was chill outside. Bone-cutting chill. But

the wind had not come yet. I left the shelter of the cottage. Its thick stone walls would be welcome again soon, but for now I was happy.

The sky was clear toward the mainland, which was ten miles away but could as easily have been a hundred. Our island was that cut off from everything. Yet on a clear day I could see the cliffs of Maine. Today they were almost sharp. I could see the ice in the bay, too. It filled the water halfway between the cliffs and the island. In between was choppy sea.

I walked around my tiny world, around and down to the edge of the rocks. Sometimes there were things to find, treasures swept in by the sea. Today there were only a few sticks of driftwood.

I bent to save them from the waves. The boys could hammer at them. The stove could eat them. I touched the sea-worn wood. My fingers curved around fantastical shapes. Or I could keep them in my room.

They'd make a lovely mermaid castle.

I turned. The sky was black to the east, cloud-black clear across the Atlantic Ocean. And nothing between the Old World and America but our island. I stared back up the mound of bare rock to the buildings. There was the bell tower for the fog bells, the boathouse for our dory, the animal shed. There sat our cottage, snug against the base of the tower. My eyes climbed the tallness of the lighthouse.

Such a lighthouse! It was a wonder. I loved its whiteness. I loved the stripe of bright red that swirled around its sides. Especially, I loved the windows at the top and the big shiny lamp within. From those windows you could see across the world. You could see into the waters. You could almost see the mermaids I knew lived in the waves. Even in winter I loved this island.

The wind tore suddenly at my cape. It was time to tend the animals. I struggled up the rough, rocky mound.

# CHAPTER TWO

# Papa's Helper

**P**apa ordered me to the lighthouse that afternoon. He'd been giving me keeper lessons. Mama used to help out with that, but with her big belly it was hard for her even to climb the steps. They *were* endless and winding. Like going up a great white tunnel. That left only me to help Papa, but I didn't mind. I loved gazing out those windows.

"Kate!" Papa's voice tore me from the view. "Keep your mind on what I'm saying. For more than a moment? *Please*."

I'd been wondering about mermaids again. What did they do in winter? Did their tails get all icy? Or did they sleep through the cold, like bears?

"*Kate!*"

"Yes, Papa." I wanted to be obedient, truly. But sometimes it was hard.

"Daughter, you must listen well. Should the light go out, lives could be lost. The ships at sea depend upon us. You must learn the work."

He had my attention now. "Must I take the solemn oath, too? About never failing to keep the lamp lit from sunset to sunrise? The way you did, Papa?"

Papa rubbed at his soft brown beard. "First you must understand." He pointed to the darkened lamp. "Tell me about it."

I studied the huge glass and brass oval. It loomed far over my head like an over-grown honeycomb. Layers of sharply pol-ished edges ran up and down its sides. "It's a Fresnel lens, Papa. Invented by Mr. Fresnel in France. With only one flame inside, it can shine like thousands of candles."

He smiled at last. His brown eyes smiled, too. "Yes?"

"And we feed the lamp with whale oil. We must keep it all very shiny and clean, so the beam can be seen by the ships at sea." I finished reciting. There, I proved I had been listening. Most of the time.

Papa swung open a small glass section of the lamp case. "Darkness is coming early with the storm. You will light the light today, Kate."

"Me?" I hesitated. "For the first time?"

"Yes," Papa agreed. "For the first time."

I stepped closer and stretched to stare into the cave of gleaming glass. It was like a wonderland. Almost as good as my mermaid world. My face reflected back at me countless times. I smiled at the images. Frowned. Smiled once more. Then I blinked and remembered myself.

"Wind the crank for the oil flow," I whispered. Done.

"Polish the glass." It was already

blindingly clean. I flicked the cloth in my hand anyway.

"Check the wick." It looked fine.

All was in readiness. Still, I waited, my body half-swallowed by the great lamp. What would happen when this cave was filled with light?

"Have you forgotten, daughter?" Papa's voice boomed behind me. It echoed around the cavern of glass.

"No, Papa."

I lit the lamp.

Blazing light dazzled me. My head spun a little. I pulled myself from the cavern and shut the door. Next I bent low, to the platform beneath the lamp. The big crank must be wound. The one that made the light revolve. Our light must protect ships in the bay, too, not only those at sea.

Finally I stood. "There, Papa."

"You remembered." He nodded to himself with some satisfaction. "Now we must brave the weather."

I shivered. The black clouds from the east had arrived. With them came harsh winds and sleet. Already the windows around our tower were icy. They had to be clear for the light beam to pass through.

"I'm afraid of the catwalk, Papa. I might slip right through the iron bars."

"Nonsense." He bundled me into my cloak. "It's safe enough. The strongest part of the tower. And the wind is not yet truly dangerous." Papa pointed to a nearby coil of rope. "But when it is, you must wear the safety line."

Papa opened the glass door to the catwalk. The wind nearly stole my cloak. I tightened the clasp and pulled up the hood. Thank goodness I didn't have to do this every night. Thank goodness Papa was here to do it for all of us. I struggled out onto the narrow walk.

The next quarter hour felt like ten. Standing on tiptoe, I scraped the panes next to Papa. All the way round, making a complete circle. Once scraped, the

windows had to be coated with glycerin. My fingers froze to the brush. Sleet peppered my face. I hardly noticed Papa stumble on something. But I caught the grin on his lips when he rose. Then he was guiding me inside, to safety and warmth.

When I could breathe again, I turned to Papa. He was still grinning. "What is it? What happened out there?"

He held up a sorry bundle of feathers. "A wayward duck has provided us with supper!"

I studied the creature. "Well, if ducks insist on flying into our windows . . ." I rubbed my frozen hands and laughed.

"Roasted duck." Papa was laughing with me. "Such a rare treat is worthy of this occasion. We'll celebrate the new assistant keeper of the light!"

My eyes widened. "Me, Papa?"

"Yes, you, Kate. You've learned your duties well, my girl. I'm pleased with you."

That was high praise, indeed. I beamed as brightly as the lamp.

# CHAPTER THREE

# Mermaids Never Go Hungry

The winds of winter swept over us for a week or two. It was normal weather for a rock in the middle of the sea. High tides brought the waves halfway up the sides of our island. My brothers were forbidden to go outdoors. They ran through the house, instead. They raced up the tower and down. Then they did it all ten times more.

Papa was sore afraid they'd make some mischief with the light. He lay down a new law.

"No more boys in the lamp room!"

The bad weather laws were fine with

15

me. I was nearly a keeper. I could sit up in the lamp room during the day. I'd gaze out the window for hours. Or work on my sewing. Or draw pictures of mermaids on the blank pages of Papa's books.

It was peaceful for a while. Papa generally slept during the day. But when he woke, he expected to see work done.

"Why isn't the brass polished, Kate? Have you been dreaming the entire day?"

"No, Papa."

"You're drawing in the family Bible, Kate? And sea creatures all over my lamp manuals?" He swept them aside. "I fear your heart is not in your labors, Kate."

Papa went to the big diary that must be kept. "Were there no ships passing today? You know we must record all passing ships!"

"But I did, Papa! See?" I pointed to the margins. "I drew everything I saw. There was a two-masted schooner." My finger moved to another spot. "And a brig—"

He looked fair to tear out his beard. "Written record, daughter. It must be written!"

"It's all there, Papa. I used your spyglass to see their names."

Papa squinted at the tiny names. They were carefully printed on the hull lines of the ships. "The *Mary Jane*?" He squinted some more. "At one o'clock of the afternoon? Sailing north?" He raised his head. "I can barely read this. How will the inspector manage?"

For myself, I thought the pictures made the dull book much nicer. I'd forgotten about the inspector, though. Papa might be right about him. I hung my head at my folly.

Papa only sighed. "You disappoint me, daughter. Go down to your mother. If you can't do the work here, you'll return to helping there. She surely needs it."

"But Papa—"

He lifted the trapdoor. My new rank was gone. I was banished.

In the kitchen I really regretted the peace I'd lost. Joel and Davey were wrestling all over the floor. The twins were crying above their yells. Mama was using her sieve on the last of the flour. She'd found quite a bit of wildlife in it.

"Look to the babes, Kate," she begged. "While I look to these weevils."

I peeked into the bowl. I'd been mostly hungry all day. Mostly hungry for a week or more. It was a hard feeling to forget. "Are you sure they're not good to eat?"

Mama rubbed wearily at her forehead with an arm. Her black hair was falling from its bun. "We've not come to that, Kate. Not yet."

"If you say so, Mama."

I picked up Patience in one arm. Then I hoisted Prudence with the other. I fell into a chair and they squirmed all over me. They were grateful for the attention. But I wasn't thinking about the twins. I was thinking about mermaids again.

I was certain there were lots of good reasons for being a mermaid. More certain than ever. First, they never lost the jobs they truly wanted. Second, they never had to look after the babies while their brothers played all day. All they had to do was swim and be happy. No one could take that from them.

But far, far more important, mermaids never went hungry. They feasted on sea flowers. And tiny shrimp. They opened oysters to suck on pearls. Pearls must be the sweets of mermaids. They didn't bother drinking salty seawater, either. When they were thirsty, they sipped on the nectar of—

Prudence shoved her fist into her mouth. She began to whimper.

"Are you hungry, Prudie? Thirsty?" Silly question.

"Joel! Stop fighting for a moment. Bring me a little warm milk. . . . Davey? Hold Patience. I'll feed Prudie first."

* * *

Papa ate his dinner very fast that night. It wasn't hard, as there wasn't much to eat. He glanced from his empty plate to Mama.

"The barometer is going up, Hope. The weather may clear tomorrow."

"Yes, husband?" Mama waited for his next words.

"If the seas look safe in the morning . . ."

Mama's face filled with fright. "You'd take out the boat?"

"I think I can make the five miles to the ice floes. Through my spyglass they seem to be breaking."

"But, husband—"

"I must get word to the Lighthouse Service, Hope. Our whale oil is running low."

I was interested in the talk, yet I kept my eyes down. I was still out of favor with Papa. If only I'd remembered to polish that brass! If only—

"We need provisions, too," Papa allowed.

My head jerked up. Would Papa brave the sea were the whale oil not low? But I'd knocked at the tanks this very morning. They hadn't sounded the least bit hollow. Could he fear to admit our growing hunger? Even to himself? I forgot to keep my silence.

"Will you be back before nightfall, Papa?"

"Weather and the Lord providing, Kate. I've never missed a night these fifteen years." He studied me. "Yet one must be prepared. Can I rely upon you, daughter? To watch over the light, just in case? Can I give you another chance? After this afternoon—"

"Oh, yes, Papa!" My heart rose within me. "I forgot myself only a little! I know what must be done if the need is great. Truly, I do!"

Mama clutched at her stomach. The new babe inside must be kicking again. "I pray the need will not be great, husband."

Papa got up, decided. "You'll take my first shift in the tower tonight, Kate. I need the extra sleep for strength. I'll leave at first light."

He bent to kiss Mama's brow. "Save the hen eggs, wife. We'll have flour enough for cake tomorrow night!"

*Cake.* I smiled. Mermaids could never eat cake. They could never keep the light in the tower, either. But I'd been given a second chance. *I* could keep the light.

# CHAPTER FOUR

# Storm!

The sun rose like one of my dreams the next morning. It glittered pink and gold over a dark blue sea. But its glitter was cold.

Standing by the boathouse, I worried strands of my long dark hair. I'd already given Papa a hand with the dory. Now the boat was sliding down its tracks, down to the sea. And Papa with it. He'd never taken that boat out in January before. In a moment the prow cut into the water with a splash. Then he was straining at the oars, growing smaller between the waves.

I searched the blue sky again. There was nothing up there but a few seagulls.

There'd never been such a clear sky in January. I mistrusted it.

"Godspeed, Papa!" I shouted.

I don't think he heard me.

Mermaids forgotten, I polished brass with a will all morning. We ate cod from the bottom of the salting barrel at midday. That left milk and eggs in our pantry. The milk was saved for the twins. The eggs were saved for Papa's cake.

Mama napped with the twins that afternoon. There was nothing left for her to cook. Even the boys began to understand. They took fishing poles to the edge of the rocks. They knew the water was too rough to catch anything. Still, they tried.

I climbed back up the tower. The tightness of its walls was comforting. This time I polished glass. I only stopped to check the horizon for ships. And to scan the bay for Papa's return.

* * *

When the wind came it was sudden. It was out of the north-northeast. First the windows shook around me. I lowered the spyglass to the sea. The waves had turned to mountains.

"Joel and Davey!" I cried.

A frantic search brought them into sight. They were scrambling up the rocks, waves nipping at their heels. Fishing poles were abandoned behind them. I prayed them safely to the cottage and heard the big wooden door slam. All the way up here in the tower I could hear the force of it.

Only then I remembered the barometer. Papa had taught me how to read it. I knew high numbers meant good weather. Low numbers meant bad. I tapped the glass tube hung between tower windows. The mercury fell. Disastrously. My heart fell with it.

Papa would not be returning. Papa could not return in such seas. I would be keeper of the light this night.

* * *

Snow came with the lighting of the lamp. Hard and thick it came. Thicker than any fog. I shuddered. The fog bells must be wound. But with this gale force wind . . . I grabbed the safety rope and dragged it down the stairs. In a moment my cloak was on.

"Kate! Where are you going?"

Mama was huddled in her rocking chair by the warmth of the stove. The little ones huddled with her. There'd been no supper for any but the babes.

"The fog bells must be wound, Mama. Our light can't get through this snow."

"I won't let you go out there, daughter. It would be your death!"

"Papa trusted me, Mama. It's my duty." I stood taller. "And I shall do it."

Mama studied my face. She knew my mind was made. "And the rope?"

"Tie it around my waist, Mama. Good

and strong. And the other end to the door. It will get me back."

"Child, child," Mama whispered. But she tied the rope, extra strong. Then she hugged me. "Go quickly."

The door smashed shut behind me. I waited for the tower beam to pass over to light my way. When it came, struggling through the snow, I gasped. The sea had passed its high mark on our island. It was but ten yards from our door. Its spray flew at me, mixing with the snow. I couldn't tarry.

The wind shoved me along. Then it was dark again, and I stumbled.

*Wait for the light. . . . Go a few feet. . . . Try to breathe.*

Between the flashes I finally made the bell tower. I hugged a post as hard as Mama had hugged me. I was grateful for it. It stood so firm against the storm. I was grateful for the rope, too. Without that tether I'd be in the sea.

With all my might I grasped the crank. I wound. I wound till I could no more. Then I waited.

*Boom!* . . . *Be-ware!*

The bell worked! It was deafening, so close. Yet it was music to my ears.

*Boom!* . . . *Be-ware!*

I waited for another clash. Then I turned.

Going back was harder than the coming. Far harder. The force of the wind was against me. The fury of the snow blinded me. I clung to the rope for dear life.

Could I make it? Would I be swallowed forever by this great storm? There'd been precious little to eat all day. Faintness was coming over me. My knees began to buckle.

Suddenly the rope tightened. I felt myself being pulled in. *Reeled* in to the house. How could that be?

My answer waited at the door. Joel and Davey stood just outside it. They were snow-covered and heaving, surrounded by coils of rope. The door clattered shut behind us. I collapsed.

"Look what we caught, Mama!" Joel shouted.

"Our biggest fish yet," Davey crowed.

I laughed. It wasn't easy, frozen through as I was. Still, I laughed. Maybe brothers weren't useless.

Outside, the fog bell boomed.

# CHAPTER FIVE

# Castaways

Sleep usually brought my welcome dreams. Now I fought against sleep and dreams both.

Huge yawns overtook me as I doused the light with the dawn. I'd never been so tired. All night I'd been in the tower. I'd only drifted asleep but once. Well, maybe twice.

Just one more look out the windows. Then bed. No mermaid bower could ever be as soft and warm as those waiting quilts. Lurching to the windows, I peered down.

Everything in the world was white.

The island's rocky mound was covered with snow. The high seas were white-capped. The sky still swirled with falling snow. Everything white, except—

My body sprang to attention. I rubbed sand from my eyes and grabbed the spyglass.

Everything was white save for a small boat washed up on the edge of the rocks. Papa? Could it be Papa's dory? Even as I watched, the waves pulled at the boat. Surely Papa would never leave his dory at the mercy of the sea.

"Mama!"

I was halfway down the winding tower steps already.

"Mama! . . . Joel! Davey!"

Mama stumbled from her bedroom. She was still in her nightgown. "What is it, Kate? What's the trouble?"

"There's a boat! A boat cast away on our rocks!"

The boys and I raced down the

island. The wind was stiff, but no longer a danger. Still, I feared the boat might be swept from us.

Where had it come from? How had it found its way to us through the storm? Was it empty? I'd seen no life aboard through the spyglass. But then, I hadn't lingered over the sight. I'd run instead.

We skidded to a halt by the boat's high bow.

"Come on, Joel. We've got to pull her to safety."

"I can help, too!" Davey shouted through the snow.

"Good!"

Together we tugged. With all our might. A fresh wave crashed into the stern, giving us some lift. We got the boat perched on a rocky ledge. I scrambled up the side and peeked in.

"Oh!"

"What is it, Kate?"

"Oh," I repeated. Was I awake? Or

was I dreaming after all? "My goodness. It's a *mermaid*. And her baby!"

Well, they had looked like mermaids lying there all wrapped in gold and seaweed. But when we got them up to the house they turned into people. Very nearly frozen to death people.

Mama and I raced around preparing hot water and a bath. Joel and Davey went back down to the water. They were hoping to scavenge something else. Something to *eat*.

My lady mermaid opened her eyes first. She was in the tin tub of hot water. Long honey hair flowed over her shoulders. She was like a beautiful, cold statue. Mama was rubbing at her hands. I was rubbing her feet.

"*Pearl*," she croaked. "Where is my pearl?"

Mama stopped rubbing. She was taken aback. "We've stolen no jewels, mistress. It's the Lord's truth!"

"More precious than jewels . . ." The lady coughed. "My child!"

Mama smiled with relief. "Not to worry your head, mistress. Your little Pearl is warm and safe."

I pointed. "Over by the stove. In the big crib. She's napping with our twins."

"Thank God!" My mermaid closed her eyes again.

As I fetched a blanket for her, the door crashed open. The boys had returned. Joel was tugging at a huge crate. Davey rolled in a smaller keg.

"What did you find?"

"Don't know," Joel huffed. "'Twas the only thing on the rocks. Downwind from the boat."

"Mine was in the boat!" Davey was pleased with himself.

Mama was shielding the lady from the boys' eyes. "Don't just stand there, the two of you. Open them!"

I jumped to pry at Davey's keg first. He poked his nose next to mine into the opening.

"What is it?"

I pulled out a rock-hard cracker. "Hardtack, I think. A whole keg of hardtack!"

"Can you eat it?"

"Yes," I smiled.

Joel's crate was more mysterious. Inside lay round orange balls, one after another. I poked one. It had a firm, waxy skin. "Mama?"

Mama bustled over. "Lord love us! I've seen them once. At Christmas when I was a child. It's a crate of oranges you've found! From the southern climes!"

Joel picked one up. "Oranges? Can you eat them, too?"

Mama grabbed at her big stomach and laughed. "Eat them? Why, they're a fruit. A treat beyond compare! We're saved, children. Kate's mermaid has saved us all!"

39

*  *  *

It was not till evening that we heard the story of my mermaids. Everyone was calling them that now, even if we did know better.

Both slept clear through the day. Clear past the lighting of my lamp. Then Mrs. Cobb told her story. For that was her name, Emily Cobb—and little Pearl, snug and smiling in her lap.

"We came from the south," she began. "In my husband's brig . . ." She paused to wipe at a tear. "What has become of him? Of his men and ship?"

"Don't fret now," Mama said. "You need your strength. Give thanks for your deliverance, and the Lord will provide."

Mrs. Cobb smiled bravely. "We were caught in the terrible storm. Worse than a hurricane in the southern seas, it was. My husband ordered the cargo overboard first to lighten the ship. Then he heard the fog bells. He feared for the ship itself. That it might be dashed on the rocks . . . He tied our baby and me into the open boat. He set us free. . . ."

"That's all I remember. Until now." Her eyes were very beautiful, even with tears in them. "Thank you for saving us."

"It was my daughter," Mama said. "Thank Kate. She's the one who's been keeping the light. And the bells, too." Mama turned to me. "You've done well, Kate."

I only smiled. My mouth was full of the sweetness of oranges. Nectar of *oranges* was what mermaids drank. I knew that for a fact now.

# CHAPTER SIX

# Keeping the Light

**H**ardtack could be filling, dunked in warm milk. It wasn't bad scrambled in eggs, either. Ground, it made a kind of porridge. Mama tried every recipe she could conceive. She had eight mouths to feed. The oranges lasted but a week. Papa was still gone after two.

The weather would not clear. The waves were still mountains. No one could get on—or off—our island.

Mrs. Cobb was good company when not weeping. She did a fair amount of that for her lost husband. Fortunately she went off to my room to do it. It was now her room. I slept up in the tower. My bundle of quilts was as warm there. And I was near the lamp.

The mermaid dreams had disappeared. My whole life had taken on a new pattern. Everything revolved around the light and the fog bells. The light must shine. At all costs it must shine.

Now when I dreamed, it was of ships in danger. Ships foundering in great storms. The masts would blow down. Angry seas would surge aboard. Just on the point of sinking with the ship, I would wake. In time to check the lamp. In time to rewind the platform for the light.

It was hard to be a keeper of the light. Harder than I ever imagined.

"You're looking worn, child."

Mama hugged me on the morning of the fifteenth day. I could say the same for Mama. Now it was an effort for her to get around the kitchen. The baby would come soon. But all of us had been born on the mainland. Mama always went there for her delivery. Then she'd come home with another babe—or two.

I knew she couldn't get to the mainland this time. I said nothing, only reached for my hardtack porridge. I stirred the grayish sludge. "It looks delicious, Mama."

"Thank you, Kate. I might try a pot of chicken soup for our supper tonight. What do you think?"

My spoon stilled halfway to my mouth. "Chicken soup?"

"Old Betsy is not laying as well as she might, and—"

"Not Old Betsy, Mama!" Each of our dozen hens was a friend. Complain though I might about their care, they'd been hard to come by. And hard raised.

"You have a better idea, daughter?"

I shook my head dumbly. Eating our hens, our *friends*, was the beginning of the end. Would the seas never calm? Would

Papa never return? I swallowed the hard-tack porridge. It had gone cold in my bowl.

I tested the flow of the whale oil after breakfast. The light had seemed a little sluggish last night. It was worse before I extinguished it this morning. My head rose from the pipe. Were the oil tanks really going empty?

Frantic, I ran down the tower, straight to the tank room at its base. I pounded on the tanks. They still weren't hollow. I slumped down, head in hand. What to do?

"What's the matter, Kate?"

I jumped. "Don't sneak up on me like that, Joel."

"Didn't sneak. Ran in like usual. You didn't notice, is all."

"Something's wrong with the oil, Joel! I don't know how to fix it!"

"That's funny. Something's wrong with Mama, too. She just went up to her bed. In the middle of the morning! Mrs. Cobb went

45

with her. Slammed the door right in my face."

"Mama?" I could handle only one problem at a time. Here were too many. "First Old Betsy, then the oil. Now Mama. And who's looking after the babies?"

"What're you mumbling about, Kate?"

"Nothing." I studied the oil tanks again. If they weren't empty, it must be another problem. A different one. My eyes followed the piping. It wandered from the tanks up the tower. "Could something be stuck in the oil pipe?"

Joel considered. "Might be. Let me look. Please? I love to take things apart!"

"But can you put them back together again?"

"You know I can, Kate!"

I had to take the chance. "All right, then. I'll just see about the girls."

Joel was already reaching for one of Papa's nearby tools. He was happy to do something at last.

\* \* \*

Davey was in the kitchen. He was playing on the floor with all three little girls.

"Look, Kate!" he smiled. "Prudie and Patience can walk now."

I snatched Prudie from too near the stove. "Keep them from the heat, Davey. They mustn't burn themselves."

"I know what to do, Kate. I'm going to play horsie with them." He neighed. "Who wants a ride first?"

Three tiny girls squealed with pleasure. They rushed to climb on Davey's back.

The boys were working hard, and Old Betsy the hen hadn't been sacrificed yet. That left but one problem. Mama.

I knocked on her bedroom door. Mrs. Cobb peeked out.

"Kate!" she exclaimed. "I've not had time to think. Be a dear and start some water boiling. Lots of water. Then bring it up. Where does your Mama keep her fresh linen? And the baby things?"

"It's happening? Now? Without Papa?"

Mrs. Cobb's face was flushed with excitement. "Babies wait on no man for their coming. We'll make do without."

"If you say so, ma'am." I ran back to the kitchen.

All the ships in the world might have sailed by that day. They sailed without a note in Papa's lighthouse diary. Without even a drawing. There was no time for the tower. There was no time to check the weather or the seas. A new baby was being born.

Everyone did their jobs without complaint. Joel found the oil problem by late afternoon. He yelled for me.

"Kate! Come here! Now!"

I raced between errands. "What is it?"

"I found the rascal!"

Joel was covered in whale oil. He beamed as he held up a sodden object.

"What is it?"

"A mouse." He laughed. "A mouse was stuck in the oil line!"

It was hard to see in the dimming light from the nearby window. I squinted. A very small mouse. My heart went out to it. "He must have been hungry, too."

Then the darkening afternoon struck me. "No! It can't be so late already! I'll have to light the light soon. Thank you, Joel. So much. But can you put it all back together again?"

"'Course." He bent over his work.

"Kate!" Mrs. Cobb was calling.

What next?

"Coming!"

I raced back up the cottage stairs. The bedroom door was open. Mrs. Cobb stood there, holding a bundle. She smiled. "You have another brother, Kate."

I peeked into the blanket. His face was red and wrinkled. He made sucking noises. "Good. The other two are becoming useful."

I walked over to Mama and bent to kiss her. "How are you, Mama?"

"Tired, Kate dear. Happy—"

Mama never got to finish. A terrible pounding came from downstairs. "Now what?" Were the girls all right? Had Davey—

I ran.

The cottage door swung open. A big, bearded man stood there. He tossed down a sack of flour.

"Papa!" I flung myself at him. "How did you ever—"

A stranger entered behind him. Another bearded man. Younger. He looked very worried.

"Tell me. Please. Have you seen anything of a shipwrecked woman and child—" He stopped as he laid eyes on Pearl.

"My daughter! Praise be! And my wife? Could she be saved, too?"

"Jason! Husband! I knew it was your voice!" Mrs. Cobb ran into the kitchen. Straight into the captain's arms.

I stood back and smiled at it all. Everything was going to be all right again.

Papa was home.

"And what about the lamp, Kate?" Papa boomed at me. "Had you no intentions of lighting it tonight?"

"Papa!" I was stricken. The day's events swept over me. How to explain?

Suddenly came the cries of the new baby from upstairs. Papa quickly counted the children milling around him. He grinned. Then he took me into his arms for a great hug.

"You've had some excitement, too. There's just time enough to meet my newest child. Then we'll light the light. You and I, Kate. Together."

"Yes, Papa."

I smiled back at him. I could sleep again tonight, all the way through. I didn't think I'd dream of sinking ships. Not of mermaids, either. A keeper of the light was too busy saving ships upon the sea. There was no time to think about what swam beneath it.

# Author's Note

One of the Seven Wonders of the World in ancient times was the Pharos lighthouse in the harbor of Alexandria, Egypt. The Pharos was considered so important to ships that its beacon fires were tended by priests. Alas, it has been gone for aeons, but people have been building aids for navigation on the seas before and since.

Sailors in early America were helped by well-placed lanterns or bonfires on a hill. But the first permanent lighthouse in this country was built in Boston Harbor in 1716. A lighthouse tower still stands on the same spot. One of the first laws passed by the first Congress of the United States in 1789 was for the establishment of what became the U.S. Lighthouse Service. The seas were dangerous, and Americans needed protection for their men who went down to it.

Over the next two centuries lighthouses of every size and shape were built around our country. The buildings, and their keepers, served faithfully until very recent times. Today most of the lights are too weak to fight against the glare of coastal cities. Radar used on ships also makes them obsolete. The Coast Guard only keeps a few of the stations in operation, and most of these have been automated.

The era of the lighthouse keeper is over, but most of our great lighthouses remain. So what's become of them? Over 255 are known to be accessible to the public, and 34 of these can be visited in our national parks. The lighthouses have turned into parks and museums, inns and private homes.

It's hard to resist the romance of a lighthouse. They're great fun to explore and climb. And when you get to the very top, when you stand by the huge Fresnel lens and look out the windows over the sea—then it's easy to dream of another time. It's easy to believe storms are coming, ships are in danger, and you are going to save the ships and their sailors with your light.

Nothing else is like a lighthouse.

# Kathleen Karr

I fell in love with lighthouses while scrambling around Barnegat Light near Atlantic City, New Jersey, when I was a child. Since then I've explored (and climbed!) nearly every lighthouse in America—from the Atlantic, to the Pacific, to the lights overlooking the Great Lakes. My fantasy is that someday I will actually live in one. My choice would be a lighthouse just like my heroine Kate lives in, on a rocky, storm-tossed island off the coast of Maine. Just think of the stories that could be written there—and the mermaids one might meet!

# Take Mom and Dad to Walt Disney World!

## Join the National Multiple Sclerosis Society's READaTHON® reading program!

### You Could Win!

**GRAND PRIZE**
A trip for 4 people to Walt Disney World!

**OTHER PRIZES**
A Girl's or Boy's Bicycle!

T-Shirts!

Video Games!

Disney Adventures Magazine Subscriptions!

Disney Books!

Gift Certificates!

Mystery Prizes!

You could win a trip to Walt Disney World or other cool prizes! You'll also help raise money to fight multiple sclerosis!

Since 1974 <u>over 5 million kids have participated</u>! It's a great way to improve your reading, help other people, and win great prizes!

IT'S FREE! NO COST! NO OBLIGATION!

Ask Mom or Dad to Call:

**1-800-FIGHT-MS** (1-800-344-4867)
for all the information.

Or visit our web site at www.nmss.org

NATIONAL MULTIPLE SCLEROSIS SOCIETY

733 Third Avenue, New York, NY 10017-3288
e-mail address: Read@nmss.org

# Enjoy More Hyperion Chapter Books!

**ALISON'S PUPPY**

**SPY IN THE SKY**

**SOLO GIRL**

**MYSTERY OF
THE TOOTH GREMLIN**

**MY SISTER
THE SAUSAGE ROLL**

**I HATE MY BEST FRIEND**

**ALISON'S FIERCE AND
UGLY HALLOWEEN**

**SECONDHAND STAR**

**GRACE THE PIRATE**

# Hyperion Chapters

## 2nd Grade

*Alison's Fierce and Ugly Halloween*
*Alison's Puppy*
*Alison's Wings*
*The Banana Split from Outer Space*
*Edwin and Emily*
*Emily at School*
*The Peanut Butter Gang*
*Scaredy Dog*
*Sweets & Treats: Dessert Poems*

## 2nd/3rd Grade

*The Best, Worst Day*
*I Hate My Best Friend*
*Jenius: The Amazing Guinea Pig*
*Jennifer, Too*
*The Missing Fossil Mystery*
*Mystery of the Tooth Gremlin*
*No Copycats Allowed!*
*No Room for Francie*
*Pony Trouble*
*Princess Josie's Pets*
*Secondhand Star*
*Solo Girl*
*Spoiled Rotten*

## 3rd Grade

*Behind the Couch*
*Christopher Davis's Best Year Yet*
*Eat!*
*Grace the Pirate*
*The Kwanzaa Contest*
*The Lighthouse Mermaid*
*Mamá's Birthday Surprise*
*My Sister the Sausage Roll*
*Racetrack Robbery*
*Spy in the Sky*
*Third Grade Bullies*